BROWNIE & PEARL

Make Good

by CYNTHIA RYLANT ❈ pictures by BRIAN BIGGS

Beach Lane Books

New York London Toronto Sydney New Delhi

Brownie and Pearl
made a boo-boo.
They ran too fast
in the house.

Now the radio does not work.
It might not work
ever again.

Uh-oh.
Someone is **not** happy!
Brownie and Pearl
have to make good.

**Brownie and Pearl
have to tidy.**

They tidy the kitchen.

They tidy the playroom.

They tidy Pearl's kitty bed
(which was only a
little untidy).

But they cannot tidy the radio.
The radio is long gone.

So Brownie and Pearl sing instead.

They sing and sing and sing.
Who needs a radio?

Someone is happy now!

Brownie and Pearl made good.

For Sacha
—B. B.

BEACH LANE BOOKS
An imprint of Simon & Schuster Children's Publishing Division
1230 Avenue of the Americas, New York, New York 10020
BEACH LANE BOOKS is a trademark of Simon & Schuster, Inc.
For information about special discounts for bulk purchases, please contact Simon & Schuster Special Sales at 1-866-506-1949
or business@simonandschuster.com.
The Simon & Schuster Speakers Bureau can bring authors to your live event. For more information or to book an event,
contact the Simon & Schuster Speakers Bureau at 1-866-248-3049 or visit our website at www.simonspeakers.com.
Book design by Sonia Chaghatzbanian
The text for this book is set in Berliner Grotesk.
The illustrations for this book are rendered digitally.
Manufactured in China
0512 SCP
First Edition
2 4 6 8 10 9 7 5 3 1
Library of Congress Cataloging-in-Publication Data
Rylant, Cynthia.
Brownie & Pearl make good / Cynthia Rylant ; illustrated by Brian Biggs.—1st ed.
p. cm.
Summary: After accidentally breaking a radio, a little girl and her cat try to make up for their mistake.
ISBN 978-1-4169-8636-2 (hardcover)
ISBN 978-1-4424-3913-9 (eBook)
[1. Behavior—Fiction. 2. Cats—Fiction.] I. Biggs, Brian, ill. II. Title. III. Title: Brownie and Pearl make good.
PZ7.R982Brm 2012
[E]—dc22
2010046230